All the King's Horses

The Story of the Budweise

Clydesdales

Painting by Sam Savitt

THE KING'S HORSES

The Story of the Budweiser Clydesdales

A Studio Book

The Viking Press
New York

Copyright © 1983 by Anheuser-Busch, Inc.
All rights reserved.
First published in 1983 by The Viking Press
(A Studio Book)
40 West 23rd Street, New York, N.Y. 10010
Published simultaneously in Canada by
Penguin Books Canada Limited

Library of Congress Cataloging in Publication Data
Price, Steven D.
　All the King's Horses.
　(A Studio book)
　1. Clydesdale horse.　I. Coleman, Alix.　II. Title.
SF293.C65P74　1983　　636.1'5　　82-17409
ISBN 0-670-22588-6

Printed in the United States of America
Set in Baskerville

Contents

This book is dedicated to
August A. Busch, Jr.,
whose love of horses,
business acumen,
and sense of tradition
have created and maintained
the Budweiser Clydesdales

"Here Comes the King..."

Foreword

For fifty years now, the Budweiser Clydesdales have been delighting generations of admirers as they pull their familiar red beer wagon in live and filmed appearances. It all started in April 1933, when August A. Busch, Jr., commemorated the repeal of Prohibition by forming the original hitch of horses and then shared the sight with the nation. Public response was so immediate and so enthusiastic that Anheuser-Busch decided to display its "gentle giants," who went on to become one of the most successful advertising and merchandising symbols in American corporate history. In 1982 the three Clydesdale hitches traveled some 60,000 miles to make more than three hundred appearances at locations across the United States, Canada, and in Puerto Rico. Millions more saw the horses in Budweiser television commercials.

The Budweiser Clydesdales have a significance and an appeal far beyond that of the corporate image they have become. At every performance and in every viewing they step out of the pages of American history, harking back to the time when horsepower was literally the means by which our ancestors traveled and transported their goods. And, in a sense, the Budweiser Clydesdales transport our generation, too. They touch off a very special feeling in all of us, evoking a sense of continuity, forging a link with America's past.

Through words and photographs, *All the King's Horses* traces the Clydesdale's own proud heritage. Descendants of the great horses that carried knights in armor into battle, members of this special breed became as prized for their eye-catching looks and high-stepping leg action as for their strength and stamina as draft horses.

All the King's Horses goes behind the scenes at Anheuser-Busch's breeding facility to show where these horses come from and how they are selected and trained for the Clydesdale hitch. You will meet the drivers and grooms and learn how the horses and their wagons are cared for at home and prepared for performances on the road.

Fifty years ago, crowds were thrilled by the appearance of the original hitch. That response continues today. When the houselights dim or word passes down a parade route, spectators hush in anticipation. Then, with thunder of hooves and a jangle of harness brass and bits, the eight giants trot into sight. Electricity fills the air, as bright as sparks from the horses' iron-shod feet. And that feeling of excitement and the cheers that follow are proof of the magnetic attraction that has drawn generations of Americans toward this very special team of horses.

"And now, ladies and gentlemen, presenting the Budweiser Clydesdales! Eight tons of champions!"

The Clydesdale

Thudding hoof and flowing hair,
Style and action sweet and fair,
Bone and sinew well defined,
Movement close both fore and hind,
Noble eye and handsome head,
Bold, intelligent, well-bred,
Lovely neck and shoulder laid,
See how shapely he is made,
Muscle strong and frame well knit,
Strength personified and fit,
Thus the Clydesdale—see him go,
To the field, the stud, the show,
Proper back and ribs well sprung,
Sound of limb, and sound of lung,
Powerful loin, and quarter wide,
Grace and majesty allied,
Basic power—living force—
Equine king—the Clydesdale horse.

—Anonymous

1.

The Creation of the Clydesdale

The four-horse chariot was the basic war machine of the Greek cavalry, and one of the first successful hitches. The charioteer controlled all four horses with one set of reins.

f we were to start the story of the Clydesdale at the very beginning, we would actually find ourselves on the Great Plains of North America, not far from where most American draft horses live today. But that was sixty million years ago, and the tiny creature called *Eohippus,* dawn horse, from which all modern horses are descended, vanished from the Western Hemisphere long before history was ever recorded. And so we shall open our story in the fourth century A.D., just as the Dark Ages were descending on Western Europe. The horse had been introduced there as a military animal, to draw chariots and carry warriors as horses had done for thousands of years in Asia and the Middle East. Since speed was more important than strength, the horses used by the Greeks and Romans were

lightly built, and if chariots required extra "horsepower," drivers simply added more horses. It would take many more years for the heavy horse to be fully developed, but already the idea of the multiple-horse hitch pulling a wheeled vehicle had become firmly established in the human mind as an impressive sight.

Until about the sixth century the ox was the traditional source of power for farming and hauling, and horses were not much used for domestic service. But oxen were slow-moving and with the invention of a new, more efficient type of wheeled plow—a device that tossed soil to the side to make a deep furrow—the limitations of using oxen became apparent. Everyone agreed that horses would be better, but there were a number of technical difficulties to be overcome.

Chariots were also used for civilian transportation. This red-figured Greek amphora of the fifth century B.C. shows a marriage procession, perhaps representing the wedding of the mythological hero Hercules and the goddess Hebe.

The breast straps that were used to harness horse pulling chariots did not enable an animal to pu its full weight against the plow at an angle tha allowed it to work most effectively. But the de sign of the ox harness was also inappropriate fo the horse, since the yoke pressed directly again its windpipe and made breathing difficult. F nally, in the eighth century, the solution arrive from Asia in the form of a collar that was esp cially designed to fit the horse's neck in such way that it could lean into the traces and real throw itself into its work. Iron horseshoes, ar other Oriental invention, gave additional tra tion, and they also protected the hooves fro cracking or breaking under the strain of work. was not long before the collar was widely used c European farms and the horse was firmly estal lished as a draft animal. (The word "draft"— "draught," the British spelling—comes from a Old English word meaning "pulling." Draft be is beer that is drawn, or pulled, from kegs or ba rels; and draft horses are those that pull vehicl or objects.)

As the horse's duties became more taxin the animal's strength became far more importa than its speed, and, accordingly, horses were s lectively bred for bulk and stamina. The proce was simplicity itself: a large mare was bred to t largest stallion the mare's owner could find. Wi any genetic luck, the offspring would be bigg than its sire and dam, perhaps growing to sixte or seventeen hands or more. (A "hand," the ur for measuring horses, equals four inches, and horse is measured from its withers to the groun Modern draft or heavy horses can measure up nineteen or more hands, while most saddle hors stand between fifteen and seventeen hands higl Since large horses were so valuable, they we given especially good care, which in turn allowe them to blossom to their fullest physical pote tial. Certain areas became noted for raising tl type of horse. Blessed with abundant and nou

This sixteenth-century French enamel shows a horse plowing a field in medieval times. Horses were much better at pulling the wheeled plow than oxen were, thanks to the invention of the horse collar.

Sixteenth-century German armor for horse and rider. The knight's sword, lance, and shield added more than 200 pounds to the weight of the rider himself, a principal reason for the development of horses of great size and strength.

ing pasturage, Flanders—a medieval country
at comprised what is today Belgium, Holland,
d northeastern France—was particularly suc-
ssful.

Agricultural advances contributed to social
d political changes in medieval Europe. Larger
eas of land that the new plow and other tools
re able to clear and cultivate created a de-
and for communal labor. Families moved
ser together so that they could share the use of

wheeled ▮ ▮ore horses to pull it,
▮ ▮ ▮tions of people and
▮ ▮ve targets for plun-
▮ ▮ in the form of the
▮ ▮ection in exchange
▮ ▮e crops, and occa-
▮ ▮town's able-bodied
▮ ▮he basis of the feu-

▮ ▮nodes of warfare
▮ ▮ses proved as use-
▮ ▮re to his serfs and
▮ ▮ fields. Until that
▮ ▮d spears the way
▮ ▮r thousands of
▮ ▮with arm power
▮ ▮. But then it was

▮ ▮ ▮ ▮olding the spear under one's
▮ and guiding the tip horizontally straight
ard an opponent's body ensured greater
uracy and the horse's considerable forward
mentum added power to the thrust. This tech-

In these sketches, Leonardo da Vinci was studying the classical high-stepping pose that artists have used for centuries to characterize the spirit and power of the horse. It is this same natural action in the Clydesdale that has helped to make it such a popular performance horse.

nique of attack called for more sophisticated equipment, which was almost immediately forthcoming. A heavier saddle, with a high, chairlike pommel and cantle, helped absorb the impact, while a thick girth kept the saddle (and rider) in place. As the cavalryman now focused his attention and his lance on a single enemy, he needed protection against the blows of others, so light leather helmets and jerkins were reinforced, first with chain-mail links and then with metal plates.

Hollywood's costume epics make much of knights in full armor blithely springing into the saddle or easily dismounting to finish off a grounded foe. The real story was actually differ-

ent. By the fourteenth century the well-dresse knight was covered head and foot by helmet an plate-armor boots, with more plate covering hi torso, arms, and legs. He wore jointed gauntlet on his hands and chain mail draped over any thing else that might be exposed. Springing in o out of the saddle was a physical impossibilit under two hundred pounds of metal, and, no surprisingly, a block-and-tackle winch or sever squires were needed to get Sir Knight onto hi steed. It was not an outfit that anyone looke forward to wearing on a hot summer afternoor and, comfort aside, if a knight in armor could b as well protected as a turtle snug in its shell, a

Two-horse chariots weren't simply earthbound vehicles. In this one, painted by the seventeenth-century Italian painter Guercino, the goddess of dawn, Aurora, is being drawn across the heavens, or, more literally, the ceiling.

horsed knight was as helpless as a tortoise on back.

The standard saddle horse of the Middle es was a light animal; judging from contempo- y manuscript illustrations, it was not much er than a pony. Such an animal was physi- ly incapable of bearing the weight of a knight armor, plus his heavy lance and shield, and tainly unable to withstand the concussive ce when a lance found its target. A larger, onger animal was essential, and Flanders was place to look. The Flemish Great Horse be- ne the mount of European chivalry, for not y could this huge animal, which stood as high

as twenty-one hands, easily carry a fully clad knight; the horse could wear steel armor of its own and still gallop into battle or a tournament. Possession of such a horse was a mark of considerable prestige both for its rider and for the overlord under whose banner he served, and, whenever possible, war-horses were captured and claimed as spoils of battle.

Buying or capturing horses did not begin to meet armies' requirements, especially when monarchs and politicians began to plan their wars, and so breeding operations were established to meet the demand. Despite the considerable expense of raising such specialized animals, gov-

21

Large horses are being shown to prospective buyers in The Horse Fair, by the nineteenth-century French artist Rosa Bonheur. This painting achieved considerable international fame for its unusually powerful interpretation of a relatively mundane subject. It is without question the most popular painting ever made of draft horses.

23

ernments encouraged their citizens to breed war-horses; a statute passed in the reign of England's King Henry VIII (a skilled horseman and tournament jouster in his youth) urged Englishmen to keep large horses for breeding and to eliminate smaller, unsuitable horses.

By the time of Henry VIII, however, armies had grown less dependent on the war-horse and his armor-clad rider. A century earlier, English archers had defeated the flower of French knighthood at the battle of Agincourt. Steel-tipped arrows fired from English longbows pierced armor and brought down horses and riders from hundreds of yards away, before French lances and swords could retaliate. By battle's end, most of the fifteen thousand French knights lay dead or wounded, and the complexion of European warfare had changed.

Another type of weaponry introduced into Europe at that time also helped to end the seeming invincibility of knights in armor. Small cannons used gunpowder, an invention from the Orient, to propel iron balls with great force. When turned against a troop of mounted knights, cannon fire caused dreadful carnage. Most useful, at least initially, in laying siege to cities and large towns, cannons captured the attention of kings and their military advisers, who diverted funds from the cavalry to establish artilleries. Hand-held firearms—first arquebuses and later lighter and more accurate muskets—had replaced crossbows and longbows by the end of the seventeenth century, and if Henry VIII had urged his subjects to raise large war-horses, subsequent monarchs wanted smaller, more agile mounts for their troops of dragoons and light cavalry. Hand-to-hand combat pitted saber against saber at arm's, not lance's, length. The days of knights in armor were over.

Like soldiers after a war, Europe's large horses returned to civilian life to join their cousins plowing the fields. About this time networks of

good roads were being established, and the need for carriage and wagon horses was increasing. The strength and stamina of the Flemish Great Horse proved to be as valuable in commerce as it had once been in battle. Hitched to large wagons, large horses hauled farm produce from rural areas to the cities, and raw materials and manufactured goods to and from mills and factories. They were also hitched to barges, and plodded slowly and steadily along towpaths beside European canals and rivers.

Following the end of the age of chivalry, large horses were used for peaceful purposes again. This early-nineteenth-century painting by the English artist John Constable shows a draft horse waiting to pull a barge along a canal.

25

This attractive pair of black Clydesdales is working a field in Garliestown, Scotland.

Large horses were crossed with lighter breeds and types to produce coaching horses. Public coaches delivered passengers and mail, while privately owned vehicles were family transportation, and the sight of four-in-hand carriages became a familiar one throughout Europe. An equally familiar sight was the coach dog. The black-and-white spotted Dalmatian was a popular breed, and for several reasons. It was swift enough to keep up with a fast-moving coach, and its light-colored body and distinctive markings made it easy to spot even during twilight hours. When a vehicle had to climb a steep hill or was stuck in mud, the dog nipped at the horses' heels to encourage them to pull harder. Dalmatians became associated with other types of horse-drawn vehicles as well, including commercial wagons and fire engines, chasing away strays that would interfere with draft horses at work and serving as guards to protect the cargo.

The importance of draft horses grew as England and other European powers expanded their interests in North America. Land had to be cleared for cultivation, and large horses provided the best means of removing giant boulders, logs, and stumps. Horse-drawn wagons and carts were as important in transporting crops and manufactured goods in the United States and Canada as they were in Europe. Wagon trains, those symbols of the American westward movement, included heavy horses in their hitches. Nineteenth-century cities boasted horse-drawn trolley cars, the first means of urban mass transportation, and no city scene was complete that did not include horses pulling a variety of vehicles. Many of the large horses that helped America to grow and prosper were members of a very special breed, the Clydesdale.

Several requirements must be met before a group of animals may properly be called a breed. Members of the group must share common physical characteristics, such as size, body features,

26

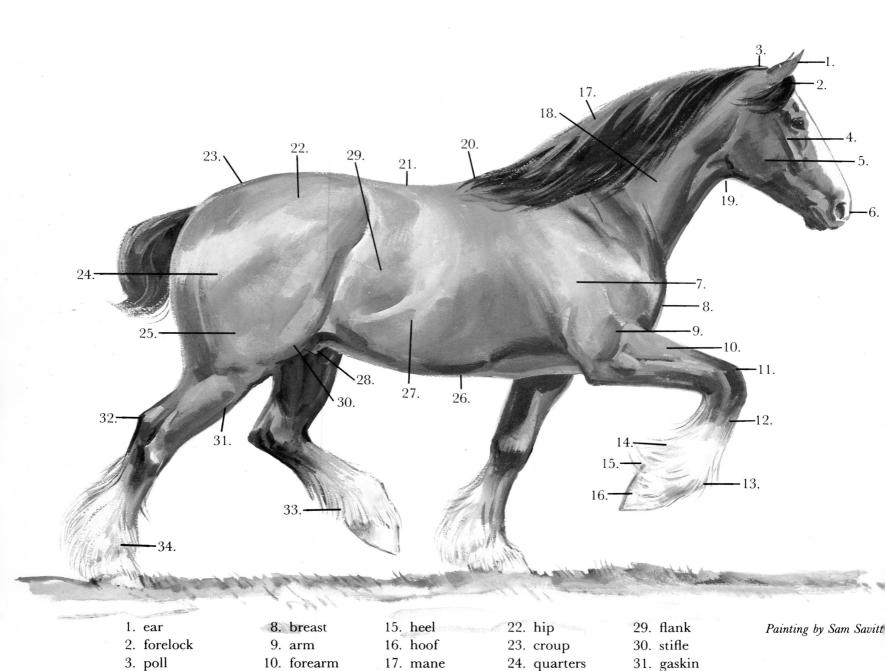

1. ear	8. breast	15. heel	22. hip	29. flank	*Painting by Sam Savitt*
2. forelock	9. arm	16. hoof	23. croup	30. stifle	
3. poll	10. forearm	17. mane	24. quarters	31. gaskin	
4. cheekbone	11. knee	18. neck	25. thigh	32. hock	
5. cheek	12. cannon	19. throatlatch	26. underline	33. feather	
6. nose	13. fetlock	20. withers	27. barrel	34. foot	
7. shoulder bed	14. pastern	21. back	28. sheath		

and perhaps distinctive color or markings. Then, too, they must be able to pass these characteristics along to their offspring. Humans help this process along by breeding only animals that possess the most desirable characteristics. The Flemish Great Horse was one example of such selective breeding; in this case the desired traits were size and gentle temperament. But the Flemish Great Horse was a type, rather than a true breed, because it did not meet a particular requirement: all members of a true breed of horses must have a known ancestry, traceable back to the "foundation" sires and dams that created the particular breed.

By the early nineteenth century, horses found in Scotland came in a variety of shapes and sizes. There were native ponies, of which the shaggy Shetland survives; light horses called "Galloway nags" were used for riding and racing. Larger still were animals descended from Flemish Great Horses that had regularly been brought to Scotland, first as war-horses and then for work. These larger horses, prized for their size and strength, were especially useful in the Clydesdale region of Lanarkshire. This region, a valley, or "dale," along the banks of the River Clyde southeast of Glasgow, contains rich farmland, and as early as the mid-eighteenth century farmers there had been successful in breeding a particularly large and strong type of horse for plowing, hauling, and carting. According to legend, one of the dukes of Hamilton, a family of wealthy landowners, had imported six black Flemish coach horses years before, stallions that he made available for breeding to local mares, and many of these horses perpetuated the new type.

Among a number of legendary equine individuals, a horse called Blaze was important in establishing this new type. His sire was a Flemish stallion brought to northern England. His dam had been stolen across the border, and by the time she was returned to her rightful owner back

The draft horses in the French painter Théodore Géricault's Cart Loaded with Kegs, *painted in 1818, bear a striking resemblance to the Clydesdales that were being developed in Scotland at about that time.*

Baron of Buchlyvie, sire of Denure Footprint, was auctioned in 1911 for £9,500 (about $55,000), a record price for a draft horse.

Benefactor, whose dam was a daughter of Denure Footprint, succeeded his grandfather as the most successful sire of show horses.

Denure Footprint was the most prolific Clydesdale stallion in the breed's history. It was said that he served mares every two hours of the day and night throughout the two weeks of the breeding season (mares were brought to him by the trainload). Foaled in 1908, Denure Footprint died in 1930.

This photograph shows excellent Clydesdale conformation features: the slightly convex "Roman" nose; a long, arched neck; and the shoulder and the pastern (the area immediately above the hoof) sloping at the same angle, allowing the Clydesdale to move its legs in its distinctive high-stepping action.

in Scotland, she was in foal to the Flemish stallion. The foal, a black colt with four white feet and a broad white stripe down his face (which suggested the name Blaze), matured into an attractive horse of 16.1 hands. Bought in 1780 as a two-year-old for the then-high price of £21, Blaze was exhibited four years later at an Edinburgh stallion show, where he won first prize, the earliest award in Scotland for the improvement of farm horses.

By the nineteenth century Blaze and other stallions had so improved Scottish horses that there was a definite draft horse variety, as distinct from the riding type. In his novel *Fair Maid of Perth*, Sir Walter Scott described a blacksmith riding a horse of the Galloway breed, while alongside rode a hatmaker on a "big Flemish mare with feet like frying pans." When referring to the latter type, people from outside Lanarkshire first called them "the Clydesman's horses," a name that was later shortened to "Clydesdales."

These early Clydesdales, though somewhat smaller than the horses we know, were far larger and more powerful than anything else available. They were said to be able to pull loads of more than a ton at a walking speed of five miles an hour, not needing to trot to accomplish that feat.

The reputation of the Clydesdales for power, endurance, and attractive high leg action soon spread beyond Lanarkshire. Some were bought by Englishmen and taken south, where they more than held their own against English horses. In a race near Bristol in the 1850s, a Clydesdale stallion owned by the Duke of Beaufort outtrotted all the other entries, including much lighter horses, over a distance of several hundred yards.

The Clydesdale Breeding Society, founded in 1877 and now headquartered north of Glasgow in Scotland, established a stud book, and the Clydesdale was officially recognized as a breed a year later. Thereafter, any horse whose entire family tree was registered in the stud book and which met certain physical standards could tech

Especially distinctive to Clydesdales are the white hair "feathers" which enhance their natural gait.

nically be called a Clydesdale. Size is one characteristic of the breed: standing over seventeen hands high when fully mature, Clydesdales possess great bulk (which horsemen call "substance"). They weigh at least 2,000 pounds and often more. They have slightly convex "Roman" noses with white "blazes," and long legs with fetlocks covered with silky white tufts of hair called "feathers." Colors can range from dark brown, nearly black, to bay and roan, which is bay mixed with white hairs. But perhaps most important, as Eric Baird, author of *The Clydesdale Horse* (London, 1982), points out:

> The Clydesdale's great attribute . . . is its stride, and this is quite exceptional. You can see it cover the ground in long strides which are graceful and light, evenly paced so that the hind hoof steps cleanly into the space flattened by the fore. This gives a good moving walk and at the trot covers quite a lot of ground, in comparison with others which may seem to be jinking along and in truth not getting anywhere much at all. Skilled driving will achieve this sort of pace and movement, although if the horse is not bred for it with the right conformation no wizard on the reins can do anything to correct it.

Clydesdales were brought to North America as early as the mid-1800s by Canadians of Scottish descent. The breed came to the United States around the time of the Civil War, and American fanciers started the Clydesdale Breeders Association in 1879, two years after the official foundation of the breed in Scotland. Although the Clydesdale was exported to many different countries, including Australia, Russia, South Africa, and Argentina, the biggest markets for Scottish Clydesdales have always been Canada and the United States.

The blustery seaside pastures in southern Scotland where these Clydesdales are raised helps them become hardy and strong. The handsome youngsters shown here belong to the Scottish breeder Jim Pickens.

Like other heavy horses, Clydesdales became an integral part of the American scene, pulling plows and other farm implements and drawing beer wagons and other vehicles. But Clydesdales were distinguished from other draft horses by their relatively finer features and eye-catching elevated leg action (especially enhanced by the white feathers). No matter how menial the task, the Clydesdale gave the appearance of quiet authority, of being a true aristocrat among workhorses.

Shortly after the turn of the century, the word "horsepower" acquired a new meaning. The internal combustion engine powered by gasoline provided an alternative method of transportation, and by the end of World War II cars and trucks had replaced horse-drawn vehicles on American roads and streets. Skeptics who had yelled "Get a horse!" at owners of Henry Ford's "tin lizzie" became believers in automotive power and reliability. As cars, trucks, and tractors nudged horse-drawn vehicles aside, it appeared that draft horses were about to become relics of the past.

This unusual photograph shows the relative sizes of four different types of horses: the Fallabella miniature horse of Argentina, the Sicilian donkey, the American quarter horse, and the Clydesdale. Note that the two larger horses are nearly the same height but that the Clydesdale outweighs the quarter horse by as much as 1,000 pounds.

Opposite: After horses pulled wagon trains full of settlers to their new homes in the American West, they were used for clearing the land, hauling, farming, and transporting the family and their produce to market.

There are more Belgians in the United States and Canada than any other draft-horse breed. Standing about eighteen hands high, the Belgian is the most direct descendant of the Flemish Great Horse, the medieval steed that carried knights into battle.

Among other breeds of draft horses imported to North America, the Shire is the largest. Often reaching twenty-one hands in height, the Shire originated in the Midlands of England.

The number of horses needed to pull a plow depended on the type of land to be cultivated. Tough, rocky soil required more horsepower.

Even more horses were pressed into service for especially demanding work. Over thirty of them pulled this harvester combine through an Oregon wheatfield in 1905.

Another draft-horse breed commonly seen in America today is the Percheron, which originated in northwest France. When fully grown, this horse measures about eighteen hands. It is a popular breed for circus performances and pulling contests as well as for farm work.

The horses in The Sand Team *by the American artist George Bellows appear eager to move their wagon away from the ocean.*

In an urban setting, this painting by the American artist Lena Gurr shows how city streets were cleared in the days before motor-driven snowplows.

Multiple-horse hitches are an enduring part of the American tradition. We've all seen replicas of the Western stagecoach, but this is a real stagecoach and its route was along Fifth Avenue, in the heart of New York City!

Students and faculty of The Ohio State University School of Veterinary Medicine made their rounds in this two-horse wagon, and so did some of the patients.

A forerunner of the subway in Brooklyn, New York, this coach was normally drawn by four horses. For a special ceremonial occasion, however, ten horses were hitched up to transport honored guests, a scene captured by H. Boese in this painting of c. 1850.

Opposite: This forty-horse hitch of Belgians, perhaps a world record number, has appeared in parades and other celebrations throughout the Midwest. Obviously, forty horses were not necessary to pull this relatively light vehicle, just as eight Clydesdales are not needed for a single beer wagon. (A draft horse worth his salt should be able to pull at least double his own weight.) But a large number of huge animals is an impressive sight—and the idea of celebrating the workhorse by giving him such a grand appearance is one of the elements in the popularity of the Budweiser image.

2.
The Anheuser-Busch Horses

In 1857, at the age of eighteen, Adolphus Busch left Mainz, Germany, to settle in St. Louis, Missouri. The son of a prominent merchant and entrepreneur, he began his career as a mud clerk on the Mississippi levee. Then, in 1859, using his patrimony, he established his own brewery supply business in partnership with Ernst Wattenberg. Shortly after marrying Lilly Anheuser, daughter of a prosperous St. Louis businessman, Adolphus was asked by his father-in-law to manage a company he had acquired as repayment for a debt, a small brewery on Pestalozzi Street, near the Mississippi River. Adolphus turned the operation into a thriving business; he was so promotion-minded that by the beginning of the twentieth century Anheuser-Busch was the country's most sucessful brewery.

Business matters aside, Adolphus Busch was personally concerned about the care the brewery horses received. When he opened a lavishly conructed, well-appointed private stable, a conmporary account outlined his philosophy:

> It has long been a pet theory with Mr.
> Busch that there was no good reason why
> an animal as clean, as orderly, and as free
> from destructive disposition as a horse,
> should not be housed as comfortably and
> with as much regard for sightliness as a
> human being. He believed that it was not
> only the humane, but the economical view,
> for long experience with hundreds of horses
> has taught him that the well-kept and well-
> treated animal does better work and more
> of it than the horse which eats, and sleeps,
> and "rests" in coldness, dampness, and
> darkness. He long ago put this theory into
> practice, and the hundreds of sleek, con-
> tented, powerful, good-natured horses
> which do the brewery work are irrefutable
> evidence of the correctness of his views.

Adolphus's son, August A., who took over the company in 1913, enjoyed spending his leisure time with and around horses. Because he too cared how the company's horses looked, he sponsored contests on Sundays in which, after a full week of heavy work, drivers of the beer wagons paraded their teams for inspection. First prize for

August Busch, Jr., driving his four-in-hand "Vigilant" coach in competition at the Devon Horse Show.

51

A turn-of-the-century Anheuser-Busch beer wagon making its rounds. The two-horse hitch was the one most commonly used for local deliveries, while a single-horse hitch (opposite) could deliver beer to more remote places. (The fly scrims over the horses' foreheads were a device to brush away insects.)

the best-turned-out team was $5, second prize $3, and third prize $2, attractive sums of money in those days. August Busch was a keen rider and "whip" (coach driver), and he relished competition whenever and wherever he came upon it. Watching a race between two horse-drawn fire engines one day, he so admired the winner that he bought the successful team and the engine, No. 9, which is on display today at Grant's Farm in St. Louis.

August A. Busch, Jr., born in 1899, inherite his family's great love for horses. He used to a company his father to the Sunday brewery-hor turnout contests, and of all the breeds he saw, was most attracted to the Clydesdales. "I like their size and their build, their feathers and the flashy, high-stepping action," he recalls. A parti ipant as well as an observer, Mr. Busch learned ride at an early age, and his adventures as young man involved almost every conceivab

nd of equestrian activity. He served as guide for ackhorse trips across the Rocky Mountains. He mpeted in such events as calf-roping, and onco-riding at Cheyenne and other rodeos, ten against his good friend, the cowboy enter- iner Will Rogers. "We both got into the buck- g-horse finals at Cheyenne," Mr. Busch relates, nd Will's horse tossed him six feet into the air. you beat me, I'll never forgive you,' Will said me. Well, I beat him, all right—my horse

tossed me *eight* feet in the air! Then we teamed up for the team roping event, and we set a record for the fastest time."

Back east, Mr. Busch played polo with and against the sport's highest ten-goal players, in- cluding the legendary Tommy Hitchcock. He rode in horse shows, including Open Jumper classes over formidable fences. He also fox- hunted regularly, riding to hounds with Pennsyl- vania's Rolling Rock Hunt, and he later served

August A. Busch, Sr., judged turn-out contests for Anheuser-Busch horses and wagons on Sunday afternoons. Cash prizes went to the teams whose horses were in the best condition and whose wagons were the most presentable.

as Master of Foxhounds for the Bridlespur Hu Club in St. Louis, which his father had founde He rode in point-to-point steeplechase races well, and when he wasn't competing on hors back, he drove Hackneys and Fine Harne horses as well as larger breeds in four-in-ha competition.

Now in his eighties, Mr. Busch continues as participant as well as a spectator. Crowds Devon and other horse shows cheer whenever enters the ring at the reins of his four-in-ha "Vigilant" to drive in coaching classes. At C mont Manor, a show and breeding stable own by his niece Sally Busch Wheeler and her hu band, Kenneth, he owns show hunters, Fine Ha ness horses, and Hackney ponies. Mr. Busch is permanent and popular fixture at New Yo City's National Horse Show, where, resplende in formal evening hunting clothes, he can be se and heard encouraging his horses and ponies.

Asked about his favorites among all the horses he has owned, Mr. Busch names two. In the 1950s he bought a show jumper named Circus Rose, which he rechristened Miss Budweiser. Mr. Busch showed the mare himself as well as lending her to the United States Equestrian Team (Arthur McCashin rode Miss Budweiser in the 1952 Olympic Games in Helsinki, Finland). "I loved that mare so much that I wanted to save the last two fences I jumped her over." And save them he did. They now stand alongside the driveway to his St. Louis home.

His other favorite was a rogue cow pony named Spot, which he successfully broke and then trained for polo and fox-hunting back in St. Louis. He once refused an offer of $25,000 for Spot, and the horse lived out his thirty years as part of the Busch family.

Mr. Busch developed his driving skills as a youngster watching the men who drove the Anheuser-Busch beer wagons around St. Louis. He often made delivery rounds with them, sitting beside the drivers and occasionally being allowed to handle the reins. Whenever possible he chose to ride on wagons pulled by Clydesdales, and when he went to work at the brewery, he took charge of the stable operation. He naturally gravitated toward Clydesdales, authorizing their purchase to join the Anheuser-Busch "fleet."

As gasoline-powered trucks gradually replaced horse-drawn wagons, opportunities to drive and direct the brewery's horses disappeared. And with the enactment in 1919 of the Eighteenth Amendment to the United States Constitution, so did the opportunity to enjoy the contents of the barrels and bottles the wagons delivered. Prohibition became the law of the land, and alcoholic beverages became illegal.

While many breweries went out of business, Anheuser-Busch switched to such products as

Trucks began to replace horse-drawn wagons as early as 1900. This 1917 photo shows part of the motor-driven fleet.

yeast, corn, and malt syrups, and other goods. August Busch, Jr., and his elder brother, Adolphus III, waited with their father for the inevitable day when Prohibition would be repealed. That day took some fourteen years to arrive, but Anheuser-Busch was ready. Minutes after midnight on April 7, 1933, the first post-Prohibition beer came out of the Pestalozzi Street brewery.

April 7 was also the day that Clydesdales became the living symbol of Anheuser-Busch. Other companies used draft horses to promote their name and their product, and once during Prohibition years August, Jr., had seen an exhibition of Clydesdales owned by the Wilson Packing Company of Chicago. Watching Wilson's six-horse hitch perform, he decided that when Prohibition was repealed, he would commemorate the event with a Clydesdale hitch.

As that day neared, Mr. Busch bought eight

A contemporary illustration of
Adolphus Busch's private stable at the
time it was opened. The building, now a
national landmark, houses the St. Louis
Clydesdale hitch on the grounds of the
Pestalozzi Street brewery.

August Busch, Sr., donating a
horse to the U.S. Cavalry, as part of
a promotion to support the American ef-
fort in World War I. Even then, the
Busch family knew that horses made for
good publicity.

The Busch family has been involved in horse sports for generations. Here, August A. Busch, Sr., is shown winning the
Park Four-in-Hand class at the 1901 St. Louis Horse Show.

desdale geldings and harness from the Union ckyards of Chicago. The horses and equipnt were secretly installed at the St. Louis wery's stables, as were former Anheuser-Busch vers Art Zerr and Billy Wales.*

In the afternoon of April 7, Mr. Busch ended his father's office. "I told him I wanted to w him a new car I just bought. My father's reion was, 'Don't you think that's a little preture—spending money for a new car when ve just gotten over Prohibition?'" But Au-t, Sr., followed his son down to the street, and a prearranged signal, a six-horse Clydesdale

team drawing a Budweiser beer wagon appeared from the distance, with Zerr and Wales in the driver's seat. "Art and Billy climbed down and hugged my father, and the three of them were crying. I cried, too, at the sight of it."

August, Jr., had other plans for the Clydesdales. Realizing the tremendous advertising and promotional potential of a horse-drawn beer wagon, he had the team sent by rail to New York City. After picking up two cases of beer that had been flown to New Jersey's Newark Airport, a six-horse hitch driven by Wales trotted through the Holland Tunnel into Manhattan. When the team pulled up in front of the Empire State Building, the beer was presented to Al Smith, former governor of New York State, who had been instrumental in Prohibition's repeal. Ac-

*Billy Wales, incidentally, was one of the most faus drivers or "whips" of his time. He had his hands ind for $50,000 and one of his Clydesdales, Sir Hubert, the most photographed horse in America.

Members of the Busch family and some friends set off for a ride. At far left is August, Sr., beside his son Adolphus III. August, Jr., is second from right.

August Busch, Jr., Master of Fox-hounds of the Bridlespur Hunt, leads hounds out for a morning's sport.

The original Budweiser Clydesdale hitch re-enacts the presentation of a post-Prohibition case of beer to President Franklin D. Roosevelt in Washington, D.C., April 1933.

cording to a newspaper account, more than five thousand people (a considerable crowd for a workday) rushed to see the presentation, and when the audience had dispersed, certain items were found to have been left behind, including seven women's shoes and a pink girdle abandoned in the middle of Thirty-fourth Street.

The Clydesdales continued on a tour of New England and the Middle Atlantic States. In Boston, the Official Greeter presented them with the keys to the city. Other stops on the tour included

Providence, Rhode Island; Manchester, N Hampshire; Baltimore; and Washington, D. where the Clydesdales paraded down Pennsyl nia Avenue to the White House to deliver a c: of beer to President Franklin Delano Rooseve re-enacting a presentation made by the A heuser-Busch Company on the day Prohibiti had been repealed.

A second hitch of Clydesdale geldings bought from the Wilson Packing Compa Driven by veteran Art Zerr, it, too, was sent

60

The original hitch outside the St. Louis brewery.

es where the hitch could most effectively mote Budweiser beer.

Once the St. Louis executives and the re al and local distributors decided on an ap ance, certain steps were taken to ensure both horses' comfort and the product's maximum act. The local Budweiser distributor began arranging the routes the hitch would take city or town officials. He also selected a wroom"—a large facility where the horses ld be stabled on public display—one with such prerequisites as sufficient space, a clean and inviting appearance, water, electricity, and good ventilation. Automobile showrooms were often used, and dealers readily agreed since they hoped that the people who came to look at the horses might also look at their cars. The local distributor was also responsible for ordering first-quality straw (for bedding) and feed: twenty-five bales of wheat straw, ten bales of timothy hay, four sacks of crimped oats, and one sack of bran to begin with; the hitch driver would later tell the distrib-

When President Harry S. Truman visited Grant's Farm in 1950, August Busch, Jr., treated him to a carriage tour.

August Busch, Jr., drives the Budweiser Clydesdales through New York City's Times Square to the 1953 National Horse Show.

or what additional supplies would be needed, pending on the duration of the hitch's stay.

Generating and coordinating publicity was other important element of a successful appearance. Window posters and other displays ed the route that the horses and wagon would ke, and in newspaper and radio announcements the public was invited to visit the showom and to watch the parade or exhibition.

Photographers were hired to take pictures of Budweiser outlet proprietors with the hitch, and a short film, *Big Scot, the Story of a Champion,* was made available to movie theaters. The local distributor was told to make sure that taverns and stores had enough beer on hand to meet consumer demand.

These procedures are followed today, under the direction of August A. Busch III, who became

Horses of the first two hitches, both based in St. Louis, pose inside their stable, now a National Historic Landmark.

chairman of the board of Anheuser-Busch in April 1977. His father, August A. Busch, Jr., is now honorary chairman of the board of Anheuser-Busch Companies, Inc. Anheuser-Busch continues to underwrite the cost of maintaining the traveling hitches and shares the cost of appearances with area wholesalers, to whom the company makes available promotion and publicity items, such as posters, bumper stickers, decals, and lapel buttons.

The medium of television provided anoth showcase for Clydesdales as the symbols of Bu weiser. *The Ken Murray Show*, an early (1950) po ular variety hour sponsored by Anheuser-Busc opened with a shot of the eight-horse hitch tro ting through the gates of Grant's Farm. TV cor mercials have subsequently featured the hitch a variety of settings and moods. Most recentl Baron, one of the Clydesdale stallions, has b come the symbol of Budweiser Light Beer, and

en galloping free through snowy fields, along a
ountain ridge, and at the seashore.

Television spawned fund-raising telethons,
d Anheuser-Busch has been an active sup-
rter of Jerry Lewis's annual Labor Day event
 muscular dystrophy; each year's poster boy or
l is photographed next to one of the hitch's
entle giants."

The publicity generated by the Clydesdales
erever they go is certainly matched by the

goodwill they inspire, and one can truly say that
while they succeed in helping Anheuser-Busch to
sell a great deal of beer every year, they have
surely transcended the role of corporate symbol.
In fact, many of the people who admire them are
neither horse-lovers nor beer-drinkers. Some fans
even consider them as much a part of the American tradition as Fourth of July parades and apple
pie. Not long ago, one of the touring hitches
picked up a CB signal from an automobile trav-

*Hitches of Sicilian donkeys and
Clydesdales in the annual New Year's
Day Tournament of Roses Parade at
Pasadena, California.*

The Clydesdales had a walk-on part in the movie Hello, Dolly! *and have appeared in other films as well, including Jerry Lewis's* Hardly Working.

Opposite: The St. Louis hitch high-steps out of the Pestalozzi Street brewery gates.

eling alongside the three trucks. "The Budweiser Clydesdales!" the man cried. "I'm so glad to see you. Now that John Wayne and Elvis have gone, you're all we have left!"

The success of the Budweiser hitch has led to much imitation, which is, of course, the sincerest form of flattery. It is true that breweries in general have always used draft-horse hitches as their

advertising symbols, but the continued popularity of the Clydesdales has inspired competitors and colleagues in other countries to keep the tradition alive. Among American and Canadian firms, Genesee and Carlsburg are identified with horses, and several British breweries, including Whitbreads, Watney, and Courage, continue to maintain horse-drawn vehicles.

To be part of the Budweiser Clydesdale operation is the dream of every young person interested in draft horses. Walt Brady, head driver of the St. Louis hitch and Budweiser's senior Clydesdale hand, comes from a Greeley, Iowa, family involved in raising and showing Belgian horses. Some years ago, Brady met Art Zerr and Andy Haxton, another driver, at various county and state fairs (he was driving a dairy wagon at the time); he told them that if a job working with the Clydesdales ever became available, he'd jump at the chance. Zerr and Haxton kept him in mind and within the year Brady received a telegram from St. Louis. He signed on as assistant groom in 1939, at the age of nineteen.

Those early years on the road were wearing, Brady remembers. Travel was by rail (truck transport was introduced in 1940). Horses, wagon, harness, and other equipment had to be unloaded from the train, then put on local trucks, then unloaded again wherever the horses were stabled. Nowadays, Brady and his colleagues transport the horses, wagon, and gear in customized tractor-trailers.

The kind of show a hitch puts on depends on the event at which it is performing. In a parade, the hitch takes its place in the procession, its Dalmatian mascot perched beside the drivers, while the handlers walk alongside, checking the equipment and keeping enthusiastic crowds from coming too close to hooves and wheels. At fair arenas and other places with room to maneuver, the hitch executes circles, figure eights, cloverleaves, and other patterns. The docking maneuver, in which the wagon is backed up against the rail and the horses moved parallel to the rail, shows spectators how barrels and cases of beer used to be unloaded while the horses stood, "parallel-parked," out of the way of traffic. The entire routine is seldom done entirely at a walk or at a sedate trot. A crowd-pleasing effect is to gallop the horses into the arena or leave in the same manner, the hitch looking for all the world like something out of the Oklahoma land rush.

Public demand for appearances, coupled with Anheuser-Busch's marketing strategy, had expanded the number of hitches to three, all based in St. Louis, by 1950, but the number was

Carrying load of three Anheuser-Busch brands, this unusual hitch has three lead horses in front of two wheelers. The photo was taken in 1955.

Opposite: Walt Brady drives the hitch through Monument Valley for a publicity photograph.

69

Always the center of attention, the hitch draws crowds to a Nebraska shopping center. It is a tribute to the good temperament of the breed that a crowd of this size did not cause the hitch horses to turn an ear!

A two-horse hitch spent the summer of 1982 at the World's Fair in Knoxville, Tennessee, where it led the daily parade held each afternoon. Also on display at the fair were new temporary stabling facilities that have been developed for the regular touring hitches to enable visitors to meet the horses face to face in their stalls.

Performing on the racetrack at the
1982 State Fair in Bangor, Maine.

72

A standard feature at the Santa Anita race track is a six-horse Clydesdale hitch, which pulls the starting gate on and off the track for all of the races. This hitch is the one that went to the World's Fair in 1982.

reduced to one later in that decade. "These things seem to go in cycles," explains August A. Busch, Jr. "I guess there was a general loss of interest in draft horses during that period. Even farmers who were using draft horses switched to tractors and trucks." But requests for appearances both from within Anheuser-Busch and from parade and fair promoters resumed, and became so numerous that in 1973 a second sta-

bling facility, the Clydesdale Hamlet in Merr mack, New Hampshire, was established adjacer to an Anheuser-Busch brewery. The Merrimac operation serves as home base for the hitch tha tours the East Coast, while the St. Louis tear covers the Midwest. A third facility, begun i 1979 and located at the Warm Springs Ranch i Romoland, California, fulfills West Coast er gagements.

The hitch in Chicago. Although the horses parade most often in small towns, big cities with their tall buildings and noisy traffic pose no threat to these experienced, level-headed animals.

A filmed sequence of the Budweiser Clydesdales passing through the gates of Grant's Farm opened The Ken Murray Show, a popular television program of the 1950s. The same scene introduced another series, The Damon Runyon Theater, and was also used in TV commercials. The musical theme that accompanied the sequence is entitled "Thracian Horse Music" (Thrace, a region of ancient Greece, was noted for its powerful chariot horses).

The photograph on the following pages was taken recently of the same classic scene yet again and has been used in magazine advertising as well as on television.

Behind the scenes in Woodstock, Vermont, during the filming of the Christmas commercial, one of the most popular Budweiser ads to date.

Take home a holiday tradition.

BRINGING YOU SOMETHING MORE THAN BEER

From the largest brewery in the world, BUD-
WEISER, which outsold any other brand of
bottled beer on Earth, brings you again the
friendly glass of good fellowship...BUDWEISER,
the King of Bottled Beer, comes to you fully
aged, fully mellowed and fully qualified to
fill once again its traditional role as the symbol
of good living, sociability and hospitality.

ANHEUSER-BUSCH • ST. LOUIS

Budweiser. ...there's nothing like it... *absolutely nothing*

One of the magnificent
EIGHT-HORSE HITCHES
of champion Clydesdale horses
used by
ANHEUSER-BUSCH, INC.,
ST. LOUIS, MO., U. S. A.
BREWERS OF THE FAMOUS
Budweiser.
LAGER BEER
and
Michelob®
DRAUGHT BEER

Photographs and paintings of the hitch quickly became an integral part of Budweiser's advertising campaigns. The magazine advertisement on the opposite page appeared as early as July 1933 and set the style for subsequent ads and tavern displays, both realistic and fanciful.

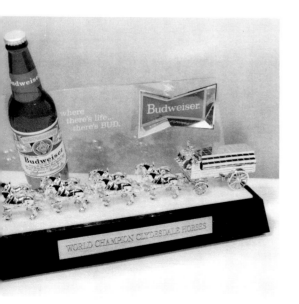

Window displays and other advertising and promotional items have always been part of the Clydesdale history as a corporate symbol. The wooden three-horse hitch was the first such item. A pewter eight-horse hitch, the definitive replica to scale, created especially for the Budweiser Clydesdales' fiftieth anniversary, is made of sterling silver, bronze, brass, and pewter.

Opposite: Baron, "star" of Budweiser Light Beer commercials. Foaled in 1977, the 17½-hand stallion was purchased in 1980 by Anheuser-Busch Breeding Farm manager Berry Farrell. The commercial showing Baron galloping across a beach was filmed in Coos Bay, Oregon; the film of Baron in the snow was made in Telluride, Colorado

Each hitch employs a crew of seven, consisting of the lead driver, his assistant, and five chauffeur-grooms, or horsemen. Although Ervin Pesek, Jr., the Clydesdale Operations manager, receives hundreds of inquiries a year about job openings, a very low turnover rate keeps such positions at a premium. Requirements include experience with horses (especially with draft horses); sufficient strength to lift the 130 pounds of harness that each horse wears; the ability to drive a big tractor-trailer; a willingness to be on the road for at least ten months out of the year; and physical and social presentability ("Our people are Anheuser-Busch ambassadors," Pesek says). Employees have come from a variety of backgrounds within the horse world: in addition to raising and showing draft horses, some have worked at racetracks and as rodeo cowboys. They

all agree that working on a hitch is a good life—not the least part of it is the benefits a driver or horseman can earn, especially with overtime pay.

Working with a hitch is far from a nine-to-five job. When an appearance is scheduled for the early morning, drivers and crew start preparing the horses long before the dawn's early light. In order to be on time for the annual Macy's Thanksgiving Day Parade, for example, the horses are cleaned and braided in northwestern Connecticut, beginning at 2:00 A.M., and then are shipped for their 100-mile trip to New York City. Evening performances done in one-day "truck-outs" may end with the horses being bedded down well after midnight. But while the crew puts in long man-hours on the job, the drivers have a strict rule to protect their horses from overwork: the Clydesdales should never spend more than four hours a day in harness.

It was relatively easy to locate and buy hitch horses in the days when there was an ample supply of draft horses to choose from. As that supply diminished, August A. Busch, Jr., developed an interest in breeding top-caliber Clydesdales, and a breeding program was inaugurated in 1940. James Kilpatrick, a leading Scottish breeder, was asked to send over eight mares, three geldings, and a stallion. Although Kilpatrick found the mares and geldings, he was unable to locate a suitable stallion before the ship sailed. The horses never reached their destination, for as the S.S. Salaria crossed the Atlantic, she was hit by a Nazi U-boat's torpedo, and the equine cargo perished. Another attempt at importing Scottish bloodstock was more successful, when in 1953 Walter Brady brought back eight mares, three geldings, and the champion stallion Commandodene.

A 1955 arrival was the twelve-year-old stallion Balgreen Final Command, who had been the first yearling colt to win the prestigious Cawdor Cup and Supreme Championship at the Glasgow Stallion Show. Balgreen Final Command proved a fine sire of both show-ring and hitch horses, including Commander, a fifteen-year veteran of the St. Louis hitch.

In 1966 Brady returned from Scotland with twenty-two mares and the stallion Bardrill Logie. Together with eighteen Canadian mares, they formed the nucleus of today's breeding program, producing thirty foals in all during their first season at Grant's Farm in St. Louis, where the company breeds Clydesdales for its three traveling teams.

The present Breeding Farm manager, Berry Farrell, grew up in Illinois, where he showed Belgians with several noted draft-horse farms. (Draft horses are shown in two divisions. The Halter division is judged on conformation, or a horse's physical qualities. The Hitch division involves performance: the horse's way of going, manners, and controllability. Hitch horses are shown singly and in pairs, fours, or sixes with carts or road wagons as vehicles.) Farrell became Breeding Farm manager in 1969 and under Mr. Busch's direction was instrumental in opening the operation to outside mares. Beginning in 1977, free service was given to approximately sixty mares a season (there is now a $200 stud fee, with a $20-a-day boarding charge).

"If it hadn't been for Mr. Busch's support," Farrell believes, "Clydesdales wouldn't have survived in the United States. He encouraged their breeding at a time when few other people had the interest or resources to do so." In addition to the free breedings, Busch instituted incentive awards, given at the National Clydesdale Show and Sales held annually at various locations in the Midwest. A $500 award went to the champion American-bred stallion and a like sum to the champion American-bred mare, with a trophy to the better of the two. Similar awards were given to Canadian-breds at Toronto's Royal Winter Fair. Begun in 1968, the awards continued for seven years, ending when Mr. Busch re-

Bardrill Glenord, noted for his outstanding conformation, was five-time champion at the Royal Winter Fair in Toronto (1969–72 and 1975) and twice champion at the National Show (1970 and 1971). Considered Anheuser-Busch's top breeding stallion to date, he sired several horses used on the Budweiser Clydesdales hitches.

Scottish breeder Hugh Ramsey and his pair of Clydesdales take Berry Farrell out into the fields to inspect his stock.

tired as chief executive officer of Anheuser-Busch, to become chairman of the board.

The breeding operation continues actively at Grant's Farm, which is in south St. Louis County. The farm, the pre–Civil War home of President Ulysses S. Grant, attracts thousands of visitors a year to its game preserves and park. Beyond the stallion barn, which is open to the pub-

lic, are pastures where Clydesdale mares and their offspring can be seen grazing and frolicking. Across the road, near Berry Farrell's home, mares in foal enjoy privacy. At times passersby can see them waiting for the foaling season and the "blessed events" that may produce possible additions to Anheuser-Busch's Budweiser Clydesdale hitches.

The next stop on Berry Farrell's annual buying trip is a farm in Fife, where Tom Brewster and his family show their Clydesdales.

89

3.
The Budweiser Clydes at Home

The horses that sire future generations of Budweiser Clydesdales live in the Stallion Barn at Grant's Farm, a popular spot with tour visitors. Television star Baron is one of the stallions on view there.

The breeding season occurs in the spring of the year, usually in April or May. The gestation period is eleven months, so that most births occur in the early spring. Twenty-eight mares were bred to seven stallions in 1981 at Grant's Farm. Consistent with the usual Clydesdale fertility rate (lower than in other breeds of horses), eighteen mares produced foals in 1982.

Berry Farrell, manager of the Breeding Farm operation, decides which mares will be bred to which stallions. The goal of breeding is to produce in offspring the best conformation qualities of the parent horses. Among those features are long cannon bones with high knees and hocks. Ideally, the rear hocks should turn inward toward each other, freeing the joints above them for the typical Clydesdale high-stepping leg action.

Berry Farrell has strong opinions about breeding only for size. "If I had a twenty-two-hand stallion, he'd attract three hundred mares a season, but you don't want to sacrifice substance and quality just for size. There's nothing wrong with a tall horse as long as breeders don't lose draftiness, the thickness of bone."

A Clydesdale foal weighs appro̶ximately 125 pounds at birth and stan̶ (when it finally gets to its feet) abou̶ three and one-half feet high. The lig̶ body coat will darken with age.

A foal spends its first six months or so at its mother's side, growing rapidly in size. When it no longer needs its mother's milk, it is weaned away to a mixture of grain and other nutrients as well as to the grass it has already begun to graze in imitation of its mother.

Colts and fillies are judged in "halter classes" and by potential buyers on their conformation features. The cream of each year's crop is kept for breeding or performance purposes, and the rest are sold.

The amount of time required for each step in the training process depends not only on the trainer's skill but also on the horse's intelligence and willingness to learn.

During a foal's first year, he is taught to wear a halter and to be led without showing resistance. Teaching a youngster to be led, although it looks simple enough, takes time and patience.

As a two-year-old, the next step in his education is to wear harness. After being fitted with the tack, the horse is turned out in a paddock and allowed to run around so that he becomes used to the feel of the harness.

After the colt becomes accustomed to wearing a full set of harness, he is hitched to a stone "boat" alongside an older, quiet, experienced mare. The boat's weight offers gentle resistance and thereby teaches the horse to lean forward into his collar. The young horse shown here has clearly not learned this lesson.

Like other horses that work, draft horses must be fitted with iron shoes to protect their feet from concussion on pavement and other hard surfaces. Clydesdales are particularly susceptible to foot ailments (it is believed that white feet are genetically weaker than those of darker colors), so special attention is given to foot and hoof care.

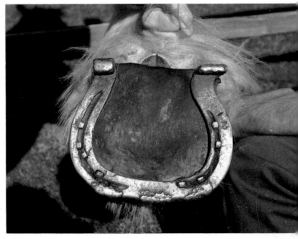

A horseshoe for a full-grown Clydesdale measures more than twenty inches from end to end and weighs about five pounds, more than twice as long and four times as heavy as the shoe worn by a riding horse. Shoes for the hind feet have tips that curve out for additional support and traction, since these feet bear the heaviest load in pulling.

A leather pad beneath the shoe protects the foot's soft sole from small rocks and other objects that might cause bruises.

Although most shoes are preshaped and then fitted to individual feet, others must be made from scratch according to centuries-old blacksmithing techniques. Here Berry Farrell works at his forge to make some new shoes for his charges.

Excess hoof growth is trimmed away, and then the shoe is attached to the hoof by eight nails, each one three to four inches in length.

A horse's hoof is made of a nerve-less, horny substance similar to the human fingernail, so that being fitted for shoes bothers the animal as little as a manicure bothers us.

Being hitched in a pair to a manure spreader teaches the young horse the finer points of being driven. Driving horses react to rein pressure and to voice commands. Berry Farrell makes sure that his horses know that being in harness means business. "I can drive two stallions through a herd of mares, and they don't become distracted in the least."

Horses are given time to relax be-
tween stages of their training. Too much
concentrated work and no play could con-
fuse or, worse, sour a young horse.

According to Walt Brady, temperament is the most important quality; a horse must be calm enough to perform in front of large crowds in different settings. Whether a horse has the right disposition is something only time will tell. Says the St. Louis driver: "Until you know what a new horse is going to do, you always wonder."

Horses that show excellent responsiveness and good temperament in harness, as well as strength and stamina, become eligible to join one of the Budweiser Clydesdale hitches. After he is moved to one of the three home bases, the horse receives additional training with one of the hitch horses before joining the team.

If a new horse doesn't already have a short, easy-to-use name, he will receive one, such as Pete, Sandy, Duke, or Barney. Big Scot, title of a short film on the Budweiser Clydesdales, has always been a popular name. Drivers shout out a horse's name to get his attention, and the horse reacts immediately.

The traditional "home" of the Budweiser Clydesdales is located on the grounds of Anheuser-Busch's St. Louis brewery, the ornate building built in 1885 as Adolphus Busch's private stable.

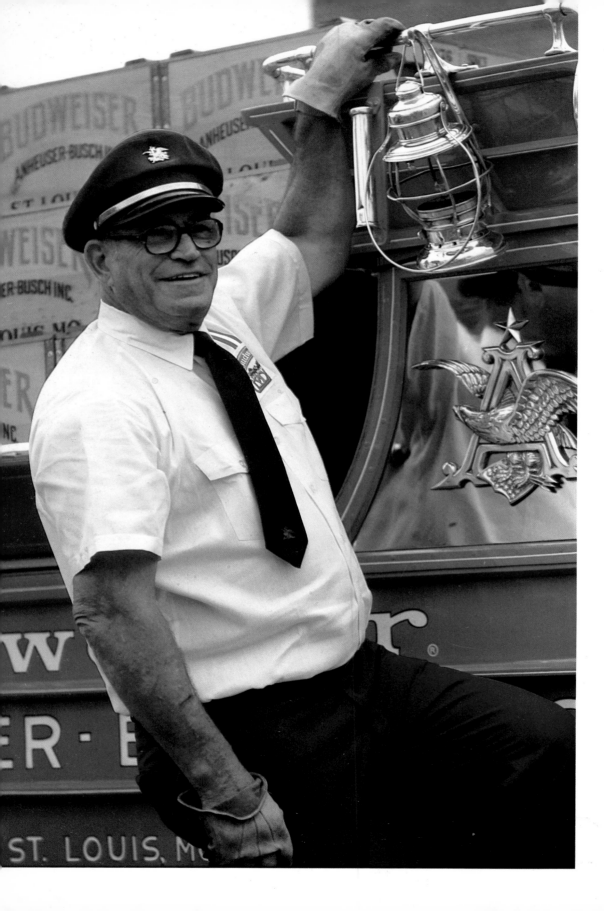

St. Louis lead driver Walt Brady joined Anheuser-Busch in 1939 as a groom on the first Budweiser Clydesdale hitch and became head driver eight years later. Walt grew up on an Iowa farm and has worked with horses all his life.

The head driver of each hitch supervises all aspects of its operation. One of his jobs is to select new horses for the team. In order to be considered, a horse must be bay (reddish-brown coat with black mane and tail) with a white blaze on the face and prominent white feet with feathers, a minimum of eighteen hands in height, and a gelding (for a more even disposition).

St. Louis hitch lead driver Walt Brady adds further qualifications. "I like my horses to stand eighteen hands at the very least and weigh at least twenty-one hundred pounds. The leaders (the front pair) should have good stepping style. The wheelers (the pair nearest the wagon) should be tall and have a lot of steam."

The lavish surroundings of the St. Louis stable make a fitting home for all the king's horses. No expense is spared to give these hardworking performers as much comfort as they deserve.

Merrimack, New Hampshire, is the home of the East Coast hitch. The Clydesdale Hamlet is modeled after the Grant's Farm Bauernhof building and courtyard in St. Louis.

Davie Pike grew up at Grant's Farm, where his father is farm manager. At the age of nineteen he went to work for Berry Farrell's breeding operation, leaving in 1979 to become a groom on the West Coast hitch. In 1981 Davie was made lead driver of the East Coast hitch.

Davie takes his team out for a tour of the Merrimack farm.

The spacious stabling facilities at Merrimack provide a luxurious home for the East Coast hitch.

The West Coast hitch is based at Warm Springs Ranch in Romoland, California.

Lloyd Ferguson, born in Minne-dosa, Manitoba, Canada, heads the West Coast hitch. He joined the Clydesdales in 1979 and became supervisor and lead driver of the West Coast hitch a year later.

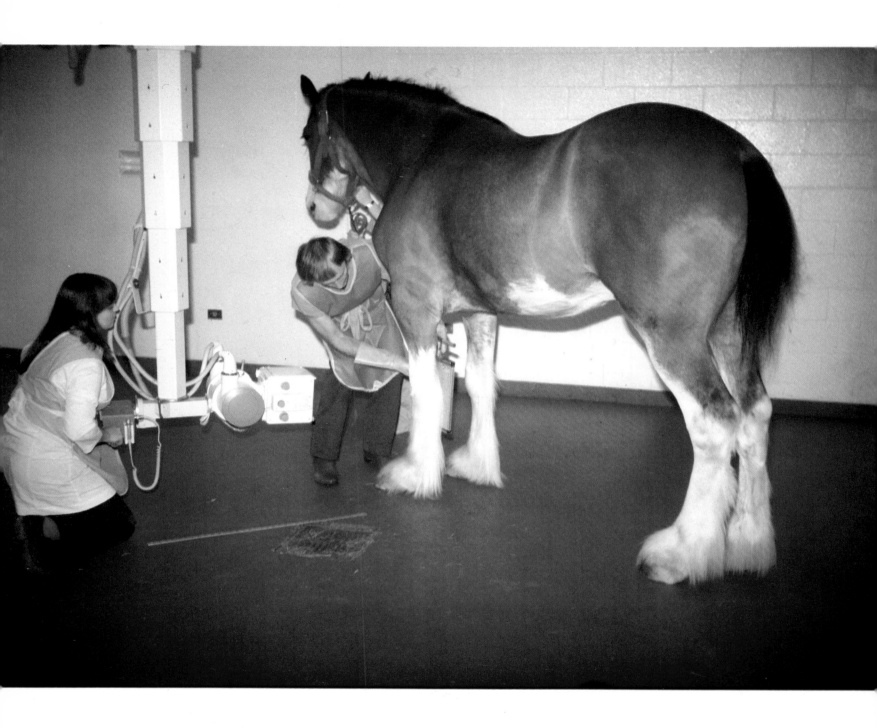

Anheuser-Busch's commitment to the well-being of its own and other heavy horses is reflected in its support of the University of Tennessee's School of Veterinary Medicine at Knoxville, a modern center for equine research and treatment.

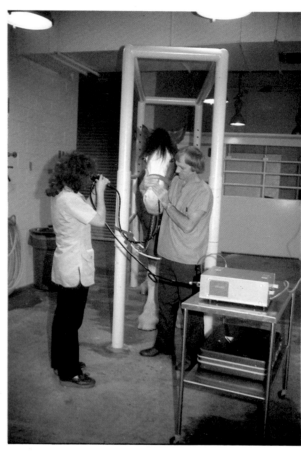

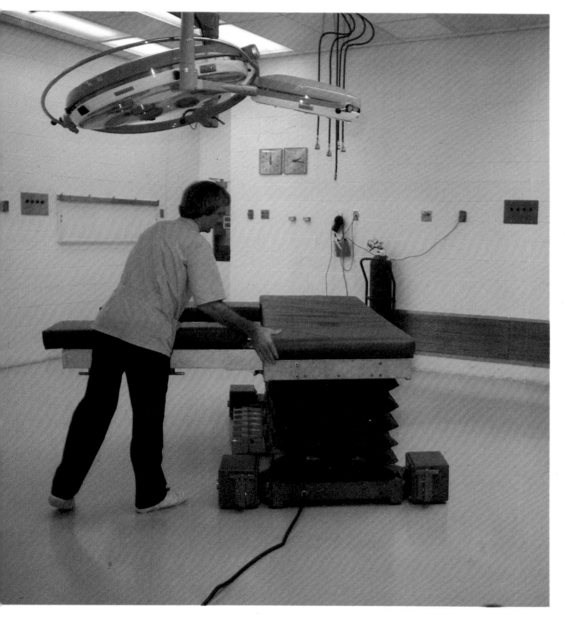

Routine health care for all hitch horses includes inoculations against equine diseases, worming, and teeth floating (filing uneven edges). Whiskers are trimmed for cosmetic reasons.

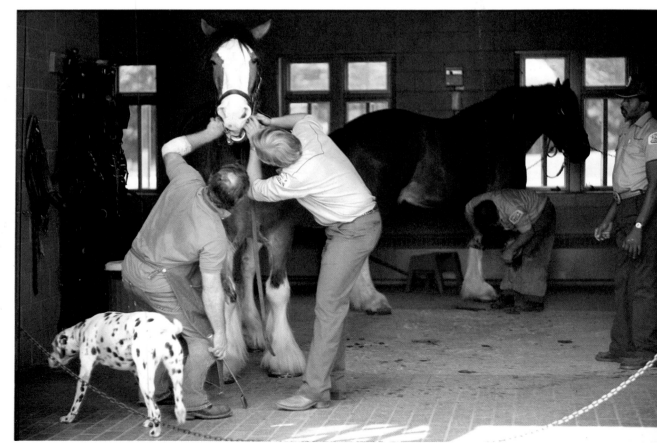

Some horses have been members of a hitch for ten years or more. When they have completed their service, they are turned out to pasture at one of the home bases or retired to Busch Gardens in Williamsburg, Virginia.

4.
On the Road

Anheuser-Busch receives more than four thousand requests a year for Budweiser Clydesdale appearances. Requests are directed to local beer distributors from parade organizers and horse-show and county-fair managers, and then coordinated through Clydesdale Operations in St. Louis. Only three hundred applications can be approved annually, but even so, each hitch travels as many as twenty thousand miles a year to fulfill engagements, and a computer system is necessary to handle the incredibly complex scheduling. Clydesdales are seen annually in the Macy's Thanksgiving Day Parade in New York City, and the New Year's Day Tournament of Roses Parade in Pasadena, California.

Most appearances are part of longer tours, which take the hitches away from home for months at a time. Others are one-day "truck-outs." Each appearance, however, requires a considerable amount of preparation.

Ten horses, eight to perform and two as extras, make up a touring hitch. The horses, wagon, crew, and equipment travel in three diesel tractor-trailers, which weigh twenty-four tons when fully loaded. Six horses ride in one truck, and four in another. Because of a hydraulic suspension system that was especially designed for the comfort of the horses, the trailer offers a smoother ride than even the cab does. The third truck, which carries the wagon and harness, travels last in the convoy to protect the horses in the event of a rear-end collision. Each truck sticks close to the next, and the drivers communicate constantly by CB radio. As they move along, other drivers keep in touch as well, asking about the horses (sometimes by name) and where the hitch will appear next.

The crew with each hitch is directed by the lead driver, but all the men pitch in to do the necessary chores, which involve care of the equipment as well as of the horses. The drivers and horsemen take special pride in their trucks as well as in their horses.

For appearances close to home, the horses are usually groomed and braided before loading.

Crossing the Canadian border, the trucks stop for the U.S. customs. Most inspectors are hard to impress, but it's difficult not to look up to a Clydesdale!

133

Once the trucks arrive, portable stalls are set up if permanent facilities are not available. Thick layers of straw are laid down for bedding, and if the floor is concrete, plywood boards beneath the straw act as an extra layer of cushioning.

The host Budweiser distributor ar-ranges for the stabling location, feed for the horses, and accommodations for the drivers and grooms.

Then the horses are unloaded, put into their stalls, fed, and watered.

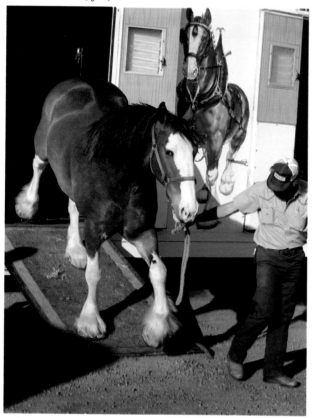

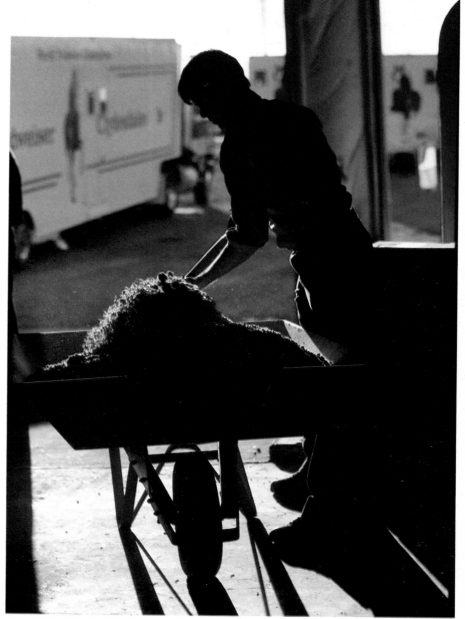

The horses are fed twice daily, early in the morning and late in the afternoon. Every day, each horse eats twenty-five quarts of feed—a mixture of crimped oats, bran, beet pulp, molasses, salt, and minerals—and fifty pounds of hay. The horses receive as much water as they wish, and they can drink up to thirty gallons daily.

138

The wagons are 1903 Studebaker meat wagons that were converted to deliver
~~er~~ (older readers will remember the Studebaker automobile, made by a company
~~~t~~ manufactured horse-drawn vehicles before shifting to cars). The wagons have
~~en~~ faithfully and painstakingly restored and are kept in excellent repair.
    The wagons have two braking systems: a hydraulic pedal device that slows the
~~hicle~~ for turns and descents down hills, and a hand brake that locks the rear
~~eels~~ when the wagon is at a halt.

A training wago

Unloading the three-and-a-half-ton wagon requires a winch. Once it has been
wered from the truck, it is pushed into the stabling area, where it will be on dis-
ay.

A detail of another wagon on display in the rotunda of the St. Louis stable.

This replica of the old St. Louis wagon was made by Al Bahr, a deaf-mute, and George Nauman. It took over two years to do the research, find the parts, and build the wagon by hand.

Whenever possible, a preparation day is scheduled the day before the hitch makes its first appearance at a particular location. Drivers and horsemen clean and polish the wagon and the horses as well.

Although the horses are thoroughly groomed every day, their legs receive speci[al] attention before a performance. They are washed with soap and water to highlight their flashy white feathers.

144

Johnny Kriz of Bethany, Connecticut, has been shoeing hitch horses for many years. The Clydesdales are reshod every five weeks, which means a lot of traveling for the farrier.

On each hitch, two grooms are assigned to the full-time job of cleaning harness. They use saddle soap to clean the leather, and then apply black shoe polish to the outside parts to produce a high shine. As with the wagon, all brass pieces are polished after each use.

Starting time is 7:00 A.M. on days when the hitch performs in the afternoon or at night. A morning performance may mean that the chores will begin shortly after midnight the night before, since the entire operation can take about five hours.

If the horses have not performed for several days, they are taken out and exercised. Some are ridden, while others are led from horseback, or "ponied." On one occasion, Lloyd Ferguson of the West Coast hitch took a break from the normal routine to do some Roman riding, with his feet placed on the backs of two horses. With some breeds this would be as risky as it is exciting, but the temperament and tractability of the Clydesdales are such that they obeyed Lloyd's commands and even leaned together to keep him firmly in place.

Even when the Clydesdales are on tour, exercising provides a welcome relief from performance duties. Just as humans enjoy a change of scenery, the horses seem to look forward to these pleasant interludes.

*Colette McGee, the only female groom, exercises three horses at once in the
paddock behind the St. Louis stable.*

Three hardworking members of the East Coast hitch enjoy a peaceful moment out of harness.

When the schedule permits, a hitch will visit a hospital, an orphanage, or an old-age home. Seeing a Clydesdale up close does much to brighten the day for patients and residents. Even more exciting is the chance to touch the horse or feed him a carrot.

Braided tails and "rolled" manes are the traditional formal turnout of Clydesdales making public appearances. The tail is divided into three sections and braided into one plait. After the end is tucked through the top knot, a shoelace is threaded through a tail needle to hold the finished knot in place.

Rolling a mane requires two five-foot lengths of cloth bunting, one red and one white. The bunting is entwined halfway down the neck in a four-strand braid, two strands of hair and two of bunting. Wire ends of crepe paper flowers are twisted into the bunting every several braids.

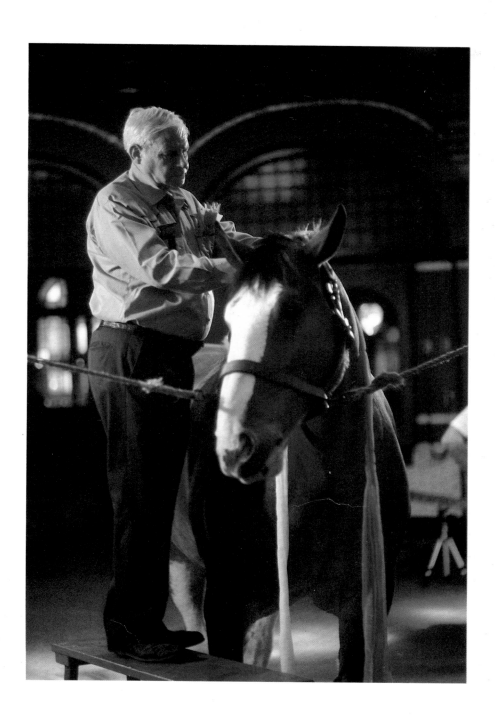

The final step is to attach a tail bow by means of a rubber band. When all the grooms assigned to the job pitch in, the eight horses can be braided and rolled in twenty minutes.

Harnessing the horses is an assembly-line operation. One at a time, beginning with the wheelers (the pair closest to the wagon), the horses are led out of their stalls to the truck that contains the harness.

The collar, with its traditional "Scotch" spire, goes on first, followed by the bridle. The bridle contains two bits, a Buxton coaching bit and a smaller overcheck that sets the horse's head carriage.

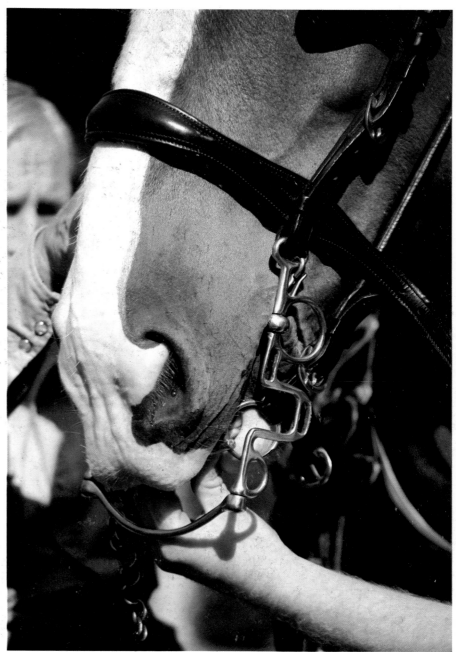

Then the back pad is buckled on and the adjustment straps tightened. The wheelers wear breeching straps, against which they lean to help back or slow the wagon.

The breast strap and traces come next, and ornamental brass martingales are put on the lead horses.

Wherever they are stabled, the Clydesdales are the center of attention. The handlers are always ready to answer questions from the large crowds that gather to admire the horses. Among the most frequently asked questions are:

- How much do the horses weigh?
  (Answer: Between 2,000 and 2,300 pounds.)

- How tall are they?
  (Answer: About six to six and one-half feet at the shoulder.)
- How much is one worth?
  (Answer: Around $10,000.)
- How much does a Clydesdale eat?
  (Answer: Twenty-five quarts of feed and fifty pounds of hay a day.)
- Why are their tails so short?

(Answer: Because their tails are "docked," or cut, so they won't become tangled in the harness.)
- Why do they have such plain names?
  (Answer: Workhorses traditionally have no-nonsense names, such as Pete, Ben, Duke, or Barney, because such names are easy for the driver to call out.)

A. browband and drop	F. bit	K. breast strap	P. back pad	T. breeching strap
B. blinder	G. bit guard	L. collar	Q. adjustment straps	U. rosettes
C. bridle	H. check holder	M. hames	R. belly band	V. tail ribbon
D. noseband	I. rein	N. rein carrier	S. breeching harness	W. quarter strap
E. check bit	J. brass martingale (lead horses only)	O. trace	(wheel horses only)	

Each set of harness weighs 130 pounds (the collar alone weighs 75 pounds) and the entire set of eight is valued at more than $40,000. Master harnessmaker John Santos of Great Barrington, Massachusetts, hand-crafts the harness from imported leather, brass, and silver. Pure linen thread is used for the stitching. An entire set of eight would take Mr. Santos more than three months of solid work to complete. The harness itself can be adjusted to fit any horse, but the collars come in different sizes and each must be fitted to the animal that wears it.

While several of the grooms harness the horses, others prepare the wagon. The wagon tongue is attached to the body, and then the swing pole and the doubletrees are buckled in place. The wheelhorses are backed alongside the tongue of the wagon, and traces running from their collars are fastened to the singletrees. The body pair comes next, then the swing team, and finally the leaders. Sets of reins buckled onto bit shanks are passed along the length of the hitch, sorted out, and looped over the wagon rail until the driver is ready to pick them up.

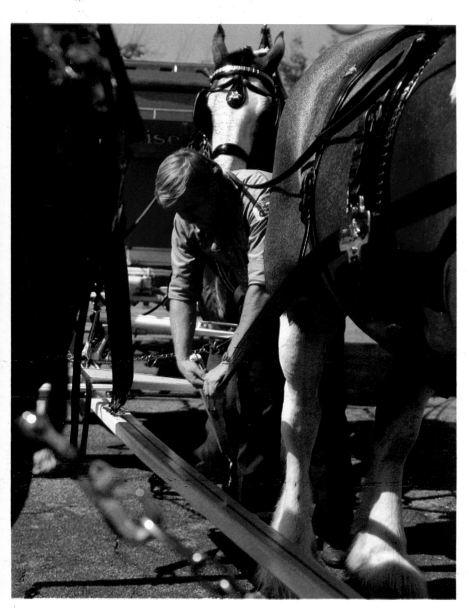

The physical ability of each horse determines his position in the hitch. Wheelhorses must be large and strong enough to start the wagon's movement and to use their weight to help slow or stop the vehicle. The swing and body pairs must be agile in order to turn the wagon. The leaders, some sixty feet out in front, must be fast, especially to carve wide, sweeping turns. Most of the horses can be worked in more than one position, and the drivers like to rotate them so that the horses become accustomed to different tasks.

The whole harnessing and hitching operation—from the moment the first horse is brought out of the truck until all eight are standing in place, ready to go—usually takes about forty-five minutes.

Meanwhile, the lead and assistant drivers have changed from their work clothes into their green uniforms.

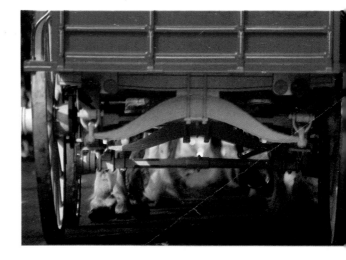

"Showtime" is now minutes away.

5.
Clydesdales on Parade

As every performer knows, waiting to go on often seems to take more time than the show itself. Happily, the Clydesdales, with their steady temperament, do not suffer from stage fright but patiently await their cue. Here they are waiting at the State Fair in Bangor, Maine.

An air of anticipation greets every hitch performance. Crowds stand in awe of the sight and sound of eight tons of Clydesdales pulling the well-known red beer wagon, then cheer as the hitch goes through its familiar yet always appreciated routine.

Driving the hitch takes strength and skill. The 40 pounds of reins that the driver holds, plus the amount of tension on the reins, totals 75 pounds (during long parades, the lead driver and his assistant will alternate taking the reins). In addition to guiding the horses with the reins, the driver shouts voice commands, getting after individual misbehavior by calling out the horse's name. If Pete, for example, is playing with his bit or leaning into the horse beside him, the driver will sternly call out his name and the horse's attention will immediately return to the job at hand.

Whenever possible, one or two members of the crew walk alongside the horses and wagon, ever alert for twisted or tangled lines or for spectators who are getting too close to the hitch.

Calgary Stampede, Alberta.

Devon Horse Show, Devon, Pennsylvania.

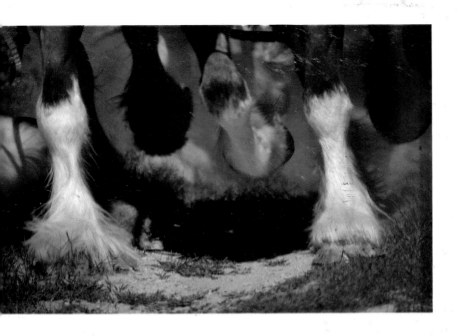

Bangor State Fair, Bangor, Maine.

The 1982 World's Fair, Knoxville, Tennessee.

Afro-American Parade, New York City.

In front of the racetrack grandstand, Calgary.

In the ring at Devon.

Yankee Homecoming Parade, New-buryport, Massachusetts.

182

Bangor.

Executing a turn at Devon.

Turning a seventy-five-foot, eight-horse hitch weighing nearly twelve tons requires skill and dexterity on the part of the driver. To execute a turn to the right, the driver pulls the set of four reins in his right hand. These reins are attached through an intricate system to the right side of each horse's bit, and the animals respond to the pressure on that side by turning right. The reins connected to the lead horses, who initiate the turn, are held in such a way that these horses receive the signal to turn before the others do.

187

Once the lead horses have turned, the other pairs follow, in sequence, in a steady rhythm and evenly spaced so that the curve of the turn is smooth.

At the Budweiser Million horse race, Arlington Park, Chicago. This figure-eight maneuver calls for twin circles, each with a diameter of some sixty feet.

The docking maneuver duplicates the way a wagon used to be positioned along a brewery loading dock in the days when hitches were used to transport beer. The hitch approaches the dock in a straight line as if moving along a busy street, swings out at a right angle to the dock, so that the wagon is perpendicular to the platform. All eight horses then step sideways in their traces without moving the wagon until they face the direction in which they came, as if "parallel-parked" to let other traffic pass by. After the wagon is loaded, or unloaded, the team swings back to pulling position and moves away.

August A. Busch III (right) and his father, August A. Busch, Jr., celebrate the St. Louis Cardinals' 1982 World Series victory at the final game in St. Louis. Television coverage was sponsored by a rival beer, and although the sponsor took a dim view of any free Budweiser publicity (in spite of the fact that Anheuser-Busch owns the Cards), the Clydesdales, together with Stan Musial and friends, were irresistibly newsworthy and made their appearance on national television.

After the performance, Bud receives a helping hand to the ground.

Following the final appearance at a location, the portable stalls are disassembled and packed. The wagon is loaded up while the horses are led into the vans.

194

On the road again.

Illustration Credits

Acknowledgments

Special thanks go to the following people, [wh]ose invaluable assistance contributed to *All [the] King's Horses:*

Mr. and Mrs. August A. Busch, Jr.

August A. Busch, III, Chairman of the [Boa]rd and President, Anheuser-Busch Com-[pan]ies, Inc.

Dennis P. Long, President and Chief [Op]erating Officer, Anheuser-Busch, Inc.

Michael J. Roarty, Vice President–Market-[ing], Anheuser-Busch, Inc.

John N. MacDonough, Vice President–[Bra]nd Management, Anheuser-Busch, Inc.

Robert D. Brandon, Director, Promotional [Pro]ducts Group, Anheuser-Busch, Inc.

Ervin J. Pesek, Jr., Manager, and Myles F. [Sni]der, Field Manager, Clydesdale Operations

William J. Vollmar, Manager, Archives [and] Records Management, Anheuser-Busch, [Inc.]

Berry Farrell, Manager, Clydesdale Breed-[ing] Farm.

Walt Brady and members of the St. Louis [hit]ch: Ned Niemiec, Don Brady, Bill Anders, [Joe] Bell, Bob Bonnarens, Colette McGee, Frank [Mon]ticello, Del Tapsell, Jim Thomas, Glenn [W]olcott, and George Armstrong

Davie Pike and members of the East Coast [hit]ch: Clyde Crum, Don Castagnasso, J. D.

Coil, Glenn Eickhoff, Steve Gottschalk, Gerald Maker, Robert Whitney, Burt Westbrook, and Archie Wycoff

Lloyd Ferguson and members of the West Coast hitch: Joe Ortega, Bill Brown, Steve Dawson, Casey Harris, John Soto, and Dennis Thompson

Peter Dunford, Elmo Johnson, and Bud Harrison of the Santa Anita/World's Fair hitch

Vicki E. Pearlman of Fleishman-Hillard, Inc.

Terry Hinkle of D'Arcy-MacManus & Masius, Inc.

Mr. and Mrs. Jim Pickens, Mrs. Nan Brewster, Mr. and Mrs. Tom Brewster, and Mr. and Mrs. Hugh Ramsey of Scotland

Aric Snyder of Interstate Studios, Sedalia, Missouri

Paul and Rob Beykirch of County Distributing Co., Inc., Sedalia, Missouri

Ken Miller of Clare Rose, Inc., Patchogue, New York

Rodney Jacobs, Peter Sellers, and the crew of Freewheelin' Films, Aspen, Colorado

Barbara Burn and Michael Shroyer of The Viking Press

Alix Coleman is a prominent horse photographer whose work has appeared in seventeen books and many magazines, including *Geo* and *Town and Country*—although she is perhaps best known as having been a principal photographer for both *Classic* and *Centaur* magazines. A large number of her photographs are on display at the Museum of the Horse at the Kentucky Horse Park in Lexington.

After studying painting at the Ecole des Beaux Arts, University of Lausanne, in Switzerland, she earned degrees at the Pennsylvania Academy of Fine Arts and the University of Pennsylvania. Ms. Coleman has photographed horse-breeding operations in many countries, including Poland and South Africa. She is a member of the American Society of Magazine Photographers and the International Alliance of Equestrian Journalists. A horseman in her own right, Ms. Coleman resides in Bryn Mawr, Pennsylvania, where she devotes her spare time to dressage.

Steven D. Price has written twelve books, nine of them about horses or horsemanship, including *Panorama of American Horses, Get a Horse!,* and more recently, *Riding's a Joy.* He was editorial director of *The Whole Horse Catalog* and is now the editor of two horse magazines, *Equisport* and *Suburban Horseman.* Mr. Price, who lives in New York City, reports on horse shows for *The New York Times* and is a member of the International Alliance of Equestrian Journalists. In the course of preparing the text for ALL THE KING'S HORSES, he interviewed members of the Budweiser hitch, both human and equine.